Jean Rogers

King Island Christmas

illustrated by
Rie Muñoz

GREENWILLOW BOOKS · NEW YORK

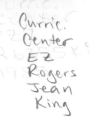

Library of Congress Cataloging in Publication Data

Rogers, Jean.
King Island Christmas.
Summary: Eskimos help a priest stranded on a
freighter in the Bering Sea to reach their island
village in time to celebrate Christmas.
1. Children's stories, American.
[1. Christmas—Fiction. 2. Eskimos—Fiction]
I. Muñoz, Rie, ill. II. Title.
PZ7.R6355Ki 1985   [E]   84-25865
ISBN 0-688-04236-8
ISBN 0-688-04237-6 (lib. bdg.)

For my own good duke, George
—J.R.

To my son, Juan
— R.M.

On King Island the wind tossed the waves higher and higher as it often does in the middle of the Bering Sea. The sun shone brightly, but in the Eskimo village on this tiny, rocky island everyone was worried.

For many months the church
had been dark and silent,
awaiting the arrival of the
new father to light the candles
and celebrate Christmas.

And now he was stranded on the *North Star,*
the big freighter anchored in the angry sea.
It was her very last trip before the winter ice
closed in around King Island.

The men of the village stood ready to take their biggest oomiak, their walrus skin boat, out to the big ship to bring the new priest home. But the waves were so high the boat would be swamped. The men could not go out on such a windy day.

The villagers were crowded into the schoolhouse to wait together and see what could be done. They knew if they could not bring the priest ashore he would have to go south with the *North Star,* and they would have to wait until the next year when the ice would be gone. Ooloranna, the island chief, talked to the ship by the radio.

When he hung up he said, "There is only one chance. The sea is calmer in the lee of the island. We men of King Island are strong. We can carry the oomiak up the cliffs and over to the other side of the island, and the *North Star* can sail around and meet us."
"Yes, yes," everyone agreed.

"We cannot let the father go south. We cannot
let him go away," shouted Eir.
"We must get him ashore," Peter cried.
"Good," Ooloranna said. "We will need ten men
to carry the oomiak across the island."
Suddenly Peter cried, "Let's all go. The strongest
can do the carrying and we will all go to meet
the father and bring him here."

Eagerly the men stepped forward
and shouldered a big oomiak.

The whole village
followed.
Up the steep side
of King Island all
one hundred and fifty
people climbed.
The mother with
her new baby,
Eir and Peter,
all the school children
with the teachers.
Everyone climbed.

On the flat top of the island the wind raged.
As they rested for a moment, the villagers looked
at one another anxiously.
They could see the *North Star* rounding the island.
But would it be calm enough on the other side for
the oomiak to reach the big ship?

Down the rocky shore everyone hurried as fast as they could. Some of the men quickly climbed into the boat and started the motor.

"Gather up all the dry grass and driftwood you can find," called Eir. "We'll build a fire."

Soon a big fire was burning. Out of parka pockets came food, and the villagers gathered around as they waited and watched.

"Look!" Yakuk shouted. "The oomiak is returning!"

Ooloranna was smiling as the oomiak drew up to the shore. "Here is our new priest," he said. "Welcome to King Island, Father Carroll."

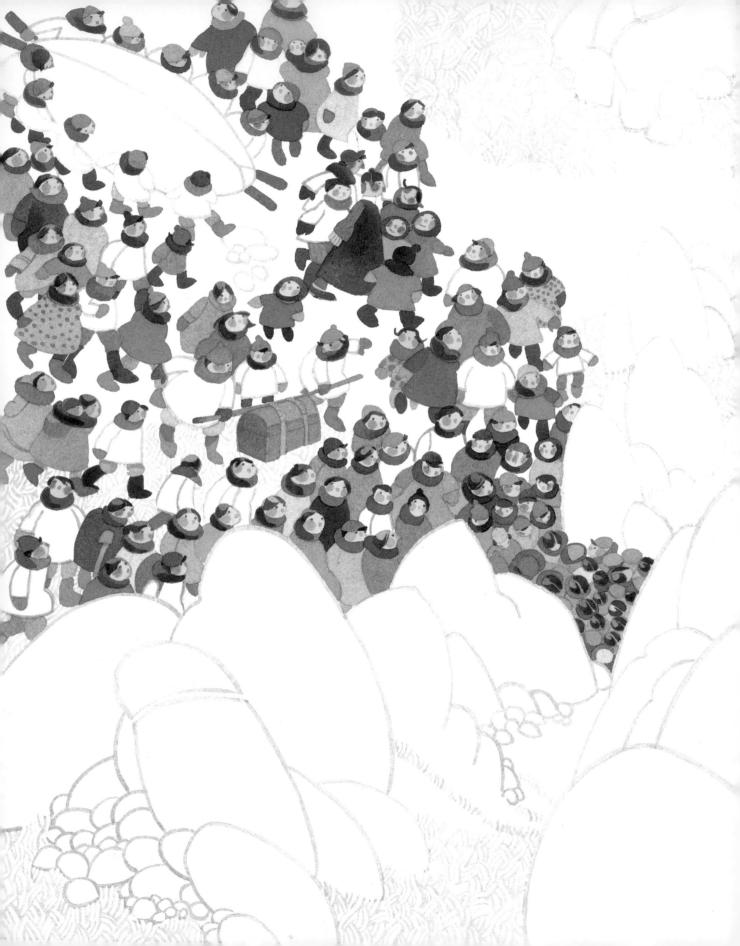

Everyone smiled as they made ready for the return trip. Up they went over the flat top of the island, laughing with the wind in their faces. Down past the graveyard to the church where smoke was rising from the chimney. Some of the older boys had hurried ahead to start the fire to welcome Father Carroll.

The Arctic ice and the days of long darkness came, but that did not worry anyone.

On Christmas Eve Father Carroll put on his most splendid robes and lit the candles in the church.

Out of the big box he had brought came warm pants and jackets, apples and oranges, and a sack of candy for everyone in the village.

The children whistled to the northern lights
to set them dancing.

There was singing and afterwards the big feast.

Christmas had come to King Island.